The Magical Door

by M. Y. Fisher

ISBN: 0-75965-228-7

1stBooks – rev. 9/24/01

*To my wife, Shona,
and to my children, Malik, Hasan,
India, and Sophia*

Once upon a time in South Philadelphia, there lived a boy named Kyle.

It was the last day of school, and Kyle and his classmates were sitting at their desks waiting for the bell to ring. Their teacher, Ms. Washington, was passing out folders to the students containing the work they had done throughout the year.

Ms. Washington set Kyle's folder down on his desk and smiled. "Kyle, you have done so well this year," she said. "Next year you will be in another grade. I'm going to miss you."

He opened his folder and leafed through the papers inside. Each page had a star on it. "You're a good student, Kyle," she said.

"You have done your best all year. Your parents must be very proud of you, their little honor student."

Kyle grinned. "I had a lot of fun learning in your class, Ms. Washington. Will you be my teacher next year?" he asked.

"I would love to, Kyle. But I have a new class coming next year, so I have to stay here. I'm sure you'll learn a lot in the fourth grade." Kyle put his head down and Ms. Washington finished passing out the folders and then collected the students' schoolbooks. The classroom walls were bare of the year's activities. Their emptiness was a sign of the end of the school year and the beginning of summer vacation.

When the bell rang, the kids yelled, "Bye, Ms. Washington!" and charged for the door. Kyle got up and started walking with his basketball and book bag. "Are you going any where special this summer, Kyle?" Ms. Washington asked.

Kyle frowned. "I don't know," he said.

Kyle met up with his friends Donald and Rasheed at the school bus stop. "Hi guys!" Kyle said.

"Hey Kyle. Guess where I'm going this summer?" Rasheed asked. Before Kyle could answer, Rasheed said, "I'm going to summer camp at Cape May. Then after camp my mother is taking me to an aquarium."

"That sounds like a lot of fun," Kyle replied.

Donald said, "I'm going to my grandmother's house for the summer. She is taking me to Buddy World Amusement Park."

"Where are you going, Kyle?" Rasheed asked.

Kyle shrugged his shoulders. "I don't know yet. I think my parents are going to surprise me." The school bus came and everyone got on.

When it stopped at his corner, Kyle got off the bus and waved to his friends. He walked up the block. His house key was tied on a shoestring around his neck. His parents both worked past four o'clock, so Kyle let himself in after school each day. He ran up the steps to his house and opened the door with his key. Then he tossed his basketball and book bag onto the floor and headed for the kitchen. He took the peanut butter and jelly out of the cabinet and made himself a sandwich. He took a quart of milk out of the refrigerator, opened it, and poured some into a glass. He took his sandwich and milk up to his room.

He sat on his bed and turned on the television set. Kyle kept all of his favorite things in his room, a chemistry set, a computer, a miniature basketball court, and a toy chest. He had a big map of the world and a poster of his favorite basketball player hanging on the wall.

Kyle heard the front door shut. His mother yelled, "Kyle, are you up there?"

"Yes mom," Kyle yelled back.

"Could you please come down here? I need you to go to the store for me."

Kyle placed his sandwich by the bed and ran down the stairs. His mother hugged him and Kyle asked her how her day was.

"It was all right, not too bad," she said. "How was your last day of school?" "My teacher Ms. Washington gave us our folders with all of our homework and test papers. She told me that I am a very good student."

Kyle ran into the living room and picked up his book bag off of the floor. He unsnapped the button and took out his folder.

"See Mom?" he said and showed her the folder. "See how good I did?"

His mother smiled as she looked at all of the papers with stars and smiley faces on them. "Very good Kyle," she said. "I'm happy to see that you did so well in school this year. Now you're going to the fourth grade. And I'm proud of you." She put the folder on the table and picked up a list and some money and handed them to him. "Kyle, I want you to go to the store and get me a few things. Here's a list of what I need."

Kyle left the house. On his way to the store, he saw Rasheed and Donald leaving for the summer. They waved to him as he walked by. Kyle planned to ask his parents if he, too, could go away for the summer.

When he arrived at the store, the owner, Mr. Anderson, asked him how he was making out with his chemistry set. "You're not planning to blow up the world are ya?" he teased.

"No way, Mr. Anderson. I just test different compounds and see how they react to certain mixtures."

"Are you going to become a scientist when you grow up?" Mr. Anderson asked.

"Yes sir," Kyle replied happily.

"Well all right, little scientist, what do you need?"

Kyle gave Mr. Anderson the grocery list, and he went to get the items. Kyle's mother had several items on her list, and Kyle knew it would take Mr. Anderson a few minutes to find them all. So, he decided to browse in the candy section. There were big barrels of candy. He dug in his pocket and took out money he saved from his allowance. Then he got a plastic bag and put two scoops of candy into it and set it on the counter.

Mr. Anderson came back with the items Kyle's mother had asked for. He put them into a plastic grocery bag and handed it to Kyle. "Here you go Kyle," he said. "Everything on your mother's list is in the bag." Kyle handed Mr. Anderson the money for the candy.

Kyle thought about Rasheed and Donald and frowned.

"What's wrong, Kyle? You look so sad."

"I want to go somewhere for the summer, Mr. Anderson. All of my friends are visiting their grandparents or going to camp, and I'm not going anywhere."

Mr. Anderson said, "Young man, I hope you get to go somewhere far away and amazing, with lots of kids, singing and dancing, and most of all, with lots of candy."

Kyle said goodbye to Mr. Anderson and left the store with a hopeful smile. He trotted off to his home. When he went inside, he saw his father sitting in a chair watching television.

"Hi Dad," Kyle said.

"Hi son," his father replied.

Kyle took the grocery bag into the kitchen and set it down.

"Mom, what are we having for dinner?" he asked.

"We're having liver, rice, and brussels sprouts," she replied.

Kyle made a funny face and said, "Yuck! I'm not eating that stuff."

"Oh yes you are, young man. You will eat every bit of your food. It will make you grow big and strong," replied his mother.

Kyle thought for a moment about Rasheed and Donald and decided to ask his mother if he could go away for the summer. "Mom, can I go to Grandmom's house for the summer?" he asked.

"No, you can't go to your grandmother's house, Kyle. She has been sick lately and has been in and out of the hospital. And besides we have a mountain of bills that need to be paid and I can't afford to send you there. This summer you're just going to have to spend time with your father and me."

Kyle sighed as he walked up the stairs to his room. He pushed the door open in anger. He thought about all of the fun that his friends would have this summer.

His miniature basketball court was hanging crooked on top of the door. He picked up the small squishy ball, aimed it, and made a clear shot. All of a sudden, a Magical Door appeared in the room. Over top of the door were letters in neon lights that said, "A Great Vacation Spot." Kyle was amazed at what he saw. The door stood in mid air and slowly opened. He carefully walked through it.

Kyle stepped into a small village with teeny houses, large donuts, a yellow sky, and water clouds with pretty colorful fishes in them. Kyle saw brightly colored flowers with only two lips. The lips were covered with lipstick.

A Figet stepped up to Kyle. "Hello little boy," he said. "My name is Cootie. Welcome to the land of Bumblebyia." Cootie opened his arms wide.

Kyle heard a noise and turned around. Many other Figets, Difaddos, and Masked People gathered to see Kyle. They all smiled at him. Kyle waved and saw more little Figets playfully jumping rope in the street. Cootie turned to the crowd. "Everyone, meet

Kyle. His birthday is today," Cootie said. Kyle raised his eyebrows. "My birthday isn't today," he whispered to Cootie.

"Of course it is," Cootie said and smiled.

Someone shouted, "Happy Birthday Kyle."

Cootie pointed at one of the Difaddos. "Bring out the cake for Kyle," he said. Let's celebrate and have a party."

A lady Figet named Miss Tuweeni stepped forward. "Since this is your birthday, we each brought you gifts to open. We hope you like them all," she said. The Figets and the Masked People gathered with gifts.

Another Figet named Junie came forward and said, "Here's a gift for the birthday boy."

Miss Tuweeni smiled at Kyle and said, "for the birthday boy."

Two other Figets also said, "for the birthday boy."

A Difaddo handed Kyle a gift and all of the Figets and Diffaddos began to sing:

"Here's a gift for the birthday boy, the birthday boy, the birthday boy.

In the box is a brand new toy, a brand new toy, a brand new toy.

Here's a gift for the birthday boy, the birthday boy, the birthday boy Here's a gift for the birthday boy and we hope that You will like it."

"Here comes the cake!" Cootie shouted.

The giant cake was two stories high with blue-and-white decorations. On top of the cake were huge candles. "Make a wish Kyle and blow out the candles," Miss Tuweeni said.

Kyle looked up made a funny face. "But I can't reach the candles," he said. "They're too high up."

Junie smiled. "That's not a problem, Kyle," he said. "We have a ladder for you to climb. You're not afraid of heights, are you?" Kyle felt as if he had butterflies in his stomach. "Yes, I'm afraid of heights. I get nervous and dizzy," he said. The Figets brought over a three-foot ladder.

Kyle looked at the ladder and said, "that ladder is too short."

"Don't worry about it, Kyle. Just step on the ladder and hold on tight," Junie said.

Kyle carefully stepped on the ladder. He was wondering how he was going to reach the candles on this too-short ladder when the ladder started rising high. The ladder stopped when Kyle reached the top of the cake.

He saw the words, "Happy birthday Kyle" on top of the cake. Also on top of the cake were eight lit candles. The candles were tall, taller than Kyle! The ladder started to move again and lifted Kyle up to the top of the candles.

He took a really deep breath and blew as hard as he could, but the candles did not go out. The Figets, Difaddos, and Masked People cheered him on.

Kyle tried again, but he could not blow out the candles. Kyle yelled down, "I can't do it. I keep blowing, but it just doesn't work."

"Try it now, Kyle," Cootie said.

Kyle took a deep breath and at the same time, the fish in the water clouds also took a deep breath. The fish helped Kyle blow out the candles.

Everyone down below cheered loudly. Kyle clapped, and then grasped the ladder. Slowly, the ladder came down until it was only three feet high again.

Meanwhile, Mecca the Evil Queen of Bumblebyia was in the Rainbow Castle. Her cape dragged as she paced the throne-room floor in her black-and-pink attire. The mask she was wearing did not hide her beauty.

Mecca was bored and wanted a challenge. She glanced out of her Magical Window to see who had come in the Magical Door. Mecca waved her hand twice over the window and said, "Oh what do we have here? A little boy who wants to have fun in the land of Bumblebyia. I can't wait to meet my new competition."

Mecca yelled, "Beebee come here. I want you this instant." The big double doors opened and Beebee, her two-headed monster, rushed in. "What do you want, my Evil Queen?" Beebee asked.

Mecca said, "Beebee, a little boy just came through the Magical Doors. He is the perfect boy for me to challenge."

"Should I retrieve him for you, my queen?" asked Beebee.

"Oh no, Beebee, let him have a moment of fun, because I have a plan for him," replied Mecca.

Kyle smiled as the Figets sliced him an enormous slice of cake. The Figets placed the cake on a very large plate and Kyle took a huge bite.

"Is the cake all nice and fluffy?" Cootie asked. "If it's not, we can bake you another one."

"It's just fine, and I don't think I could eat the whole thing," Kyle said.

While Kyle was enjoying his cake, a wacky clown asked Kyle if he could show him some magic tricks.

"Sure!" Kyle said. "I'd love to see some tricks."

The clown, Doe Doe, pulled out a deck of cards and said, "Here, pick a card."

Kyle picked a card. It was an Ace of Clubs. Doe Doe shuffled them. "Put your card back in the pile," he said, and Kyle put the card back into the pile. Doe Doe shuffled the cards again. The clown took a King of Hearts from the deck.

"Is this your card?" asked Doe Doe.

Kyle shook his head. "No, that wasn't it."

The clown picked a Ten of Diamonds. "Is this your card?"

Kyle shook his head again. "No that wasn't it, either."

The clown scratched his head as if something were wrong. Then he chose a Five of Spades and asked, "Is this your card?"

"No," Kyle said. "You're not even close."

Doe Doe shrugged his shoulders. "I give up. Let me do another trick for you."

Doe Doe put away the cards, and took out a coin. He put his hands behind his back and shifted the coin from hand to hand. Then, he kept the coin in his left hand and said, "Guess which hand the coin is in."

Kyle chose the left hand. Doe Doe opened his hand there it was. Doe Doe laughed. He looked embarrassed. He said, "let me try this again."

Once again he showed Kyle the coin and then put his hands behind his back. He shifted the coin from his left hand to his right hand and then stuck his hands back out. "*Now* guess which hand the coin is in," he said.

Kyle gave it a bit of thought, and then chose Doe Doe's right hand. Doe Doe threw his head back and laughed. "Oh I don't believe this. You got it again," he said. "You're good, Kyle."

"Thank you," Kyle replied, obviously very proud of himself.

Then a kangaroo, a skunk, and a koala bear came up to Kyle. The skunk smiled and introduced himself. "Hi. I'm Smelly the skunk, and this is Leapy the kangaroo, and Beanie the koala bear."

"Hi," Kyle said. "My name is Kyle."

Smelly the skunk said, "Kyle, we would like you to be our friend."

"Sure," Kyle said. "We can all be friends."

The Figets, Masked People, and the Difaddos all gathered together for a potato sack race. Cootie asked Kyle if he would like to be in the race. Kyle smiled and replied, "Sure, that would be great!"

"Could I be in the race too?" asked Doe Doe.

"Yes," Cootie said. "Go to the starting line. It's about to begin."

"Come on hurry, hurry," Junie said and motioned the contestants in the race to move to the starting line.

Leapy the kangaroo, Smelly the skunk, Doe Doe the clown, two Difaddos, three Figets, and Kyle all lined up at the starting line in their potato sacks and waited for Junie to give the signal.

Junie said, "On your knees get ready to sneeze, *ha* choo."

They all jumped in their sacks and headed toward the finish line. Leapy was in the lead, but Kyle was right behind him. Doe Doe and a Figet followed behind Kyle. As they approached the finish line, everyone became really excited.

Suddenly, Leapy tripped and fell and Kyle crossed the finish line first. Everyone watching the race cheered when Kyle won.

Junie yelled, "Now let's get ready for the pogo stick race."

They all put down their potato sacks and picked up their pogo sticks. As Kyle, Leapy, Smelly, Doe Doe, three Difaddos and two Figets reached the starting line, Junie said, "On your knees get ready to sneeze, *ha* choo." Then the pogo sticks were in motion. They all bounced and bounced, but the Difaddos broke their pogo sticks when they jumped on them.

It didn't really matter who won, though, because they were all having too much fun.

Once again, Kyle crossed the finish line first. Junie shouted, "Kyle wins again!" Everyone cheered for Kyle.

They were all having a great time cheering, singing, and dancing when a loud slam echoed throughout Bumblebyia. Everyone in the village paused for a moment and looked around, but then quickly went back to their fun.

"What was that loud noise?" Kyle asked Cootie.

"Oh that," Cootie said. "It was nothing, just the door closing."

"There's a way you can open the door back up, right?" Kyle asked nervously.

Cootie shook his head. "No. Once the door is closed, it's closed forever."

Kyle opened his eyes wide. "No!" he shouted. "It can't be! I thought this was just a vacation."

"Some vacations are longer than others," Cootie replied. "Sorry, Kyle."

Kyle felt his heart racing. "I can't stay here," he said. "There's no TV, no camp, no arcade, no computer and definitely no chemistry set. And, if I stay here, I'll never see my family and friends again. Cootie, *please* tell me how to get back home again."

"Are you brave?" Cootie asked.

"I think so. Why do you ask"?

"Well, you're about to go on a journey that may send you home, or keep you here forever."

"I don't understand," Kyle said. "What do I have to do?"

"You have to go to the Rainbow Castle where the Evil Queen Mecca rules." "You have an evil queen?" Kyle asked. "Is she ugly and scary?"

"No, but let me tell you something about her. Mecca was an orphan child when she came to Bumblebyia. She was very beautiful. We made her our queen. When she became queen, she possessed the magic of the Rainbow Castle and the Magical Door. However, the other kids in Bumblebyia did not like Mecca. They used to tease her and laugh at her. In time she became evil and mean to all of the children who came to Bumblebyia. Once they entered, she closed the door. Then Mecca selected three of her favorite games to challenge the kids. If they won, they could go back home. But if they lost, they had to live locked up in a prison forever. So far, she has never lost. Mecca is unbeatable. But don't let that discourage you, Kyle. Try not to be afraid."

"What kind of games does Mecca play?" Kyle asked.

"I'm not sure," Cootie said. "But the chance that someone will win is slim. But if it happens, a rainbow of many colors will fill the sky."

"Wow, I have to beat the Queen in a few games in order to go back home?"

"That's right Kyle."

"This is more exciting than I thought. But Cootie, where is the Rainbow Castle anyway?"

"It's not far from here, only two blocks away. You'll find your way I'm sure."

"Well, I guess I should be on my way," Kyle said.

"One more thing, Kyle," Cootie said. "On your journey to the Rainbow Castle you have to collect all the candy you find, but don't eat any of it. Trust me, you do not want to eat the candy."

"You mean I have to carry the candy with me and not eat it?"

"Yup," replied Cootie, nodding his head.

"Wow, no kid has never done that before, ever."

"This is really important Kyle. You can't eat any of this candy for any reason whatsoever. You have to control your candy cravings even if you're really hungry. The candy is special. If you beat Mecca, the candy will set you free. If you eat the candy before the games, Mecca automatically wins."

"You'll cross a glass bridge when you get there you get to the Rainbow Castle," added Miss Tuweeni, who had been listening to Kyle and Cootie's conversation.

"Wait! Kyle, don't go without me!" shouted Doe Doe.

Beanie looked at Smelly and Leapie and said, "Kyle, we want to go too."

Kyle smiled. "Okay," he said. "Let's all go to the Rainbow Castle."

So Kyle and his friends began their journey to the Rainbow Castle. They walked along Noodle Path, but at the end there was a red brick wall in front of them. The wall was very high and very long. They saw a Diffaddo on a swing near the wall. Kyle looked at his friends and said, "How are we gonna get over this brick wall? It's much too high to climb."

Leapy said, "I bet I could jump over the wall." Leapy took a few steps back to get a running start. He ran and jumped high, but he didn't make it over the wall.

Smelly shook his head and said, "Maybe I can dig under it."

"No," Kyle said. "That will take too long."

Then Kyle came up with a plan. He went over to the Difaddo on the swing and introduced himself. "Hi, Mr. Difaddo. My friends and I need to get over that wall. If we sit on the swing, could you push us high enough to get over?"

The Difaddo got off the swing and said, "Get on and hold on tight. I'll give you a great big push."

Kyle look at the wall again and asked, "Do you know what's over the brick wall, Mr. Difaddo?"

"I'm afraid I don't. I've never been over that wall before."

Smelly stepped forward and said, "I'll go first." Smelly sat on the swing, and the

Difaddo began to push. Smelly went higher and higher. The Difaddo pushed really hard and shouted, "Jump off now!"

Smelly sailed high into the air and yelled, "Wee!" Smelly let go and went over the brick wall.

Beanie stepped up to the swing. "Please let me go next. That looks like a lot of fun." Kyle nodded, and Beanie got on the swing. Beanie was so small that the Difaddo only had to push him twice. Beanie let go of the swing on the second push and sailed over the wall.

"Now it's my turn to get on the swing," Doe Doe said.

Doe Doe got on the swing and the Difaddo began to push it. The Difaddo pushed the swing four times and then told Doe Doe to jump. However, Doe Doe was having a lot of fun and didn't want to get off the swing. Kyle and Leapy yelled, "Let go!" The Difaddo pushed him one more time and Doe Doe let go and jumped over the wall.

Kyle looked at Leapy and said, "You go before me, Leapy. I'll go last."

Leapy smiled at Kyle. "Okay, Kyle," he said.

Leapy hopped on the swing and the Difaddo started to push, but Leapy was a bit too heavy.

The Difaddo shrugged his shoulders. "I can't get him high enough."

Kyle said, "I'll help you get him high enough." So Kyle and the Difaddo pushed three times and Leapy let go and sailed over the wall.

Kyle looked at the Difaddo and said, "I hope there's a big soft pillow to land on when I go over that brick wall."

The Diffaddo laughed and Kyle jumped on the swing. "Here we go," the Diffaddo said. He only had to push Kyle three times before Kyle was high enough to let go and sail over the wall. "Wee!" Kyle shouted.

However, there was no fluffy pillow on the other side of the wall. Kyle landed in the

Great Taffy Lake. He made a tremendous splash when he landed and came up covered in sticky goo.

He looked around him and saw his friends still in the lake, covered in goo.

Smelly said, "Hey Kyle, we're in the Great Taffy Lke, isn't it fun?"

Kyle squinted his eyes and made a funny face. "Yuck," he said. "Let's get out of here."

They all swam to the edge of the lake and climbed out. "My arms are sticking to my sides," Kyle said.

"And my legs keep sticking together," added Smelly.

"So are mine," said Beanie.

"I'm sticky all over," Kyle said. "This is gross!"

As they tried to walk, a huge gust of wind carried them high into the air. Kyle and his friends sailed through the air and got stuck on the side of the house.

"Help us! Somebody get us down!" Kyle yelled.

"I can't move," Leapy said. "How are we gonna get down from here?"

Beanie looked as if he might cry. "We'll be stuck up here forever."

Suddenly, the house door opened and a mouse came out with a very large spatula. The mouse said, "I'll get you down." The mouse used the spatula to scrape them down. One at a time they fell to the ground.

The mouse looked at them sitting on the ground and said, "Hi! My name is Diddy. This is my house you were stuck to. Are you all okay?"

Kyle stood up and said, "Yes, we're fine. But we're on our way to the Rainbow Castle. Could you tell us which way we should go?"

Diddy pointed and said, "Surely. It's that way. You'll see a big pretzel. May I ask why you are going to the Rainbow Castle?"

"I'm going to the Rainbow Castle to challenge the Evil Queen Mecca," Kyle explained.

"The Queen has met her match, because Kyle will beat her in the challenge," added Beanie.

"Well," Diddy said. "I heard that she's the best. No one has ever beaten the Queen. But I sure hope you do. Good luck."

"I have to win or I'll be here forever," said Kyle. "Besides, I'm still sticky from the Great Taffy Lake. Look, I'm walking like a robot."

They all laughed at Kyle, who was walking very stiffly. Then, when they tried to walk, they realized that they walked like robots too and laughed even harder. They all laughed until they cried.

But the Evil Queen Mecca was not laughing as she sat in the Rainbow Castle and waited for them. She was working on a scheme to beat Kyle in the games.

"Beebee come here at once," she demanded. Beebee ran through the big double doors. "Yes my beautiful Evil Queen," Beebee said. "What do you need?"

"Set up the games for Kyle and me. I want to have everything ready for him when he gets here, if he gets here. His journey will not be easy. I want the non-sculls to guard the Crazy Cave, so, Kyle will not enter into the Rainbow Castle with the candy."

Meanwhile, Kyle and his friends waved goodbye to Diddy and continued their journey to the Rainbow Castle.

Smelly said, "Kyle you're a special boy and a wonderful friend to us.

We believe you will beat the Evil Queen."

Kyle said, "I'm glad to have you as my friends. Before I entered the Magical Door, I had no where to go for the summer. And all of my friends at home went away for the summer, so I was all alone. Bumblebyia is the best place I have ever been to, and you are all the greatest!"

As Kyle and his friends trotted down Noodle Path, Kyle smelled candy in the air.

They walked over to the Candy Garden, and Kyle spotted all the candy glittering on a bush. Kyle said, "Wow! This must be the candy Cootie was talking about."

Kyle picked a handfull of candy from the bush, and stuffed it in his pocket.

Leapy watched him and said, "Do you think that's enough candy?"

"I sure hope so, because I have no where else to put more candy," Kyle replied.

Leapy said, "You can put some in my pouch."

"Oh, that's a good idea, Leapy," Kyle replied. So, they began to put the candy in Leapy's pouch. Kyle felt his stomach growling. He hadn't eaten anything since he had his birthday cake. "I'm hungry," he said. "I'm just going to eat one piece."

THE MOOKY BOOKY TRIBE

NONSCULL

MECCA

Smelly shouted, "No, Kyle! You must not eat the candy. Remember what Cootie said. If you eat the candy, Mecca wins and you'll have to stay here forever. You have to play against the Evil Queen in her games. You need to win to activate the candy. Then the doors will open and you can go home."

Doe Doe frowned and said, "Kyle, go ahead and eat the candy. I don't want you to go. Stay here with us."

"He can't stay here," Beanie said. "Kyle has to finish school."

Kyle looked at Beanie. "You're right. I'm not going to eat the candy. I have to think about winning the games against the Evil Queen so I can go home."

Mecca looked into the Magical Window and saw Kyle, Leapy, Beanie, Smelly, and Doe Doe on their way to the Rainbow Castle. "I'm going to scare the pants off of them," she said. "Let's see how frightened they'll be when they see this!"

Mecca used her magic to make a giant crab appear behind Kyle and his friends. The crab crawled in back of them without making a sound. They walked along for a while not realizing the crab was behind them. Finally, Kyle said, "I feel like we're being followed."

"No, we're not being followed." Doe Doe said.

However, Kyle was certain something was behind them. "I don't want to look behind us, but I know something's there," he said.

Then Kyle noticed a large shadow that did not belong to any of them.

Kyle spun around and saw the giant crab. He yelled, and his friends turned around and saw the crab. They all screamed and ran as fast as they could. But the giant crab was fast and followed very close behind them thrashing its giant claws. They screamed some more and tried to get away from the giant crab's claws. The crab snapped his claw above Leapy's head.

Suddenly, a firefly named Bulby swooped down and Kyle and his friends climbed on his back. Bulby gently lifted them into the air. They held on tightly as Bulby flew away. Kyle breathed a deep sigh of relief. "We're saved from that giant crab," he said.

Bulby's light flashed in the sky. Kyle saw pretty fish swimming in the beautiful water clouds. When Bulby soared close to the clouds, Kyle stretched out his hand and touched the water clouds. Beanie did the same. "Wow," Beanie said. "I wish I had wings to fly like this. It's beautiful up here."

Smelly agreed. "I'd trade my stinky smell or my rock collection for a pair of wings," he said.

Leapy shook his head. "I don't want to trade a thing. I would look pretty stupid with a pair of wings," he said. Kyle laughed as he pictured Leapy, a kangaroo, with wings.

The giant firefly glided and plunged into a water cloud. The water in the cloud washed the stickiness from the Great Taffy Lake off of Kyle and his friends. When they flew out of the water cloud, Bulby flew down and gently landed so Kyle and his friends could climb off. The gang waved goodbye to Bulby as he flew away. Then they all continued walking along Noodle

Path. When Kyle spotted the big pretzel in the middle of the road, he remembered what Diddy said and knew he was going in the right direction.

Smelly sat down and said, "My feet are hurting. Let's take a rest." So the friends all sat down to rest for a bit.

Three big, mean ducks named Duba, Hickey, and Neil approached them. One of the mean ducks asked, "What do we have here, a five-course meal? My name is Duba, and this is Hickey and Neil, and we're hungry." Hickey looked at Kyle. "You look very tasty," he said. Doe Doe, Smelly, Beanie, and Leapy were frightened. Doe Doe began to panic. "Please don't eat me," he cried. "I just learned how to juggle and do tricks."

Kyle walked toward Hickey. "Leave us alone. Ducks don't eat other animals or kids or clowns."

Duba gave Kyle a hungry look and said, "We eat anything we feel like eating, especially little kids."

Kyle remembered the candy in his pocket. "Wait a minute," he said. "I have some candy. Maybe if you eat a piece, you won't be so hungry."

"We don't want any candy," Duba said angrily. "We want a delicious pot of skunk, kangaroo, koala, clown and kid stew."

Neil rubbed his large stomach with his wing and said, "Ooh that sounds so good. I can almost taste it."

Kyle looks at Smelly and whispered, "Smelly, make a stink bomb quick!"

Smelly was about to cry. "I can't do it. I tried already and it won't work." Beanie says, "We have to do *something*. They're going to eat us!"

Kyle whispered, "We're going to make a run for it."

Duba looked at Hickey. "Get a pot," he said. "We're about to have dinner."

Kyle looked at his friends and said, "Now! Run for it!" So, they began to run from the big mean ducks.

"Stop our dinner from running away!" Duba yelled, and he and the other ducks started to chase Kyle and his friends.

"Run as fast as you can!" Kyle said. "Hurry! They're gaining on us." Leapy, Doe Doe, Smelly, and Beanie ran as fast as they possibly could.

"We're going to get you and eat you all up," Duba yelled.

"You can't eat what you can't catch!" Kyle shouted. But the mean ducks were right behind them. Luckily, Kyle and his friends stumbled upon the Never-Come-Back River.

Smelly had heard about the river. He said, "We have to jump on the pegs, and if we fall, we'll never come back."

Leapy looked as if he might cry. He said, "This is it. We're duck dinner." "Come on," Kyle said. "Let's jump on the pegs and get to the other side." Leapy knew, however, that the Never-Come-Back River was the most frightening river in Bumblebyia. Many of the kids who were planning to challenge Mecca never made it to the Castle, because they fell off of the pegs in to the river. But Kyle and his friends were determined to cross the Never-Come-Back River, more determined than anyone Leapy had ever met. They carefully jumped across on the pegs, one after another, but the mean ducks were close behind.

The gang made it about half-way across the river, but they were very scared. Jumping on the pegs in the Never-Come-Back River was terrifying. They worried that they were doomed one way or another. Either the ducks would catch them or they would fall off a peg.

Duba, Hickey, and Neil were jumping on the pegs and catching up. However, Hickey jumped on the same peg as Duba, and one of Duba's huge webbed feet slipped forward. Both Duba and Hickey plunged into the Never-Come-Back River. Neil got so scared, he turned around and headed back.

Kyle, Beanie, Leapy, Smelly, and Doe Doe made it safely across the river. They stopped for a few minutes to catch their breath and then they started to walk down another path. They saw lots of houses shaped like bottles.

"Let's get a closer look," Kyle said. "I would like to see who lives in those houses." They walked closer to the bottle-shaped houses and saw eight three-foot tall babies coming toward them. Kyle was admiring the houses when Baby Number One said, "Hello."

Still shaken up from meeting the mean ducks, Kyle and his friends screamed at the sight of the babies.

Baby Number One winced and said, "Sorry we scared you like that. We're the Boo Bop Babies, and we love to sing and dance."

Baby Number Five said, "If you're hungry, we have milk, teething cookies, and baby food."

Kyle shook his head. "That's okay, no thanks," he replied. "But I would really appreciate it if you could tell us what path we're on."

Baby Number One said, "You're on Boo Bop Baby Avenue."

Kyle said, "I'm sorry for being so rude. My name is Kyle, and this is Leapy, Smelly,

Beanie, and Doe Doe. What are your names?"

The babies all looked at each other. Then Baby Number One said, "We don't have any names. There is no one here to name us. I'm Baby Number One, and this is Baby Number Two. He is Baby Number Three, and he is baby Number Four..."

Kyle put up his hands and said, "Okay, I get the picture. You all need names."

Kyle thought for a moment and then he began to name them. "Baby Number One, your name will be Jimmy. Baby Number Two, your name is Tyrone. Baby Number Three, your name is Charles. Baby Number Four, your name will be Miles. Baby

Number Five, your name will be James. Baby Number Six, your name is Larry. Baby Number Seven, your name will be Harry. And Baby Number Eight, your name will be Butch."

The Boo Bop Babies looked at each other and smiled. Jimmy said, "Thank you very much, Kyle, for giving us names. Now we would like to sing and dance for you." The Boo Bop Babies picked up their big rattles from the ground and began to sing and dance in their diapers. Kyle smiled as they danced with the rattles. The Boo Bop Baby Avenue sign lit up as the Boo Bop Babies danced under it. Kyle and his friends enjoyed the show. The Boo Bop Babies all put their rattles down and came together to form a pyramid.

Just then, Doe Doe spotted the Mooky Booky tribe coming their way. He told the others what he saw.

"We have to go," Kyle said.

The Boo Bop Babies got down from their pyramid stance. "We'll help you get away Kyle," Jimmy said. Kyle, Leapy, Beanie, Doe Doe, and Smelly said goodbye to the Boo Bop Babies, and then they started to run. The Boo Bop Babies ran to get their big milk bottles. The Mooky Booky tribe charged after them. The Boo Bop Babies held their bottles up. The Mooky Booky tribe stopped right in front of them. The Boo

Bop Babies sprayed them with milk, and then they hit them with their rattles.

Kyle and his friends climbed high up some colorful blocks and got away. They walked about a mile along the same path they had been on before, but they weren't sure if they were going the right way. Kyle saw a giant peacock named Thelma. His friends had all seen Thelma before and said she was very nice. Kyle thought Thelma was amazing. She had beautiful large colorful feathers.

Kyle approached Thelma. "Hi," he said. "My name is Kyle, and this is Leapy, Smelly, Doe Doe and Beanie. The peacock introduced herself. "My name is Thelma, and I'm very pleased to meet you all."

Kyle said, "We are lost. We can't find our way to get back on the path to the Rainbow Castle. I have to challenge the Evil Queen Mecca or I can never go home again."

"The Evil Queen is very mean to the children who come to Bumblebyia. She is mean to the animals who live here too. She wants to pluck all my feathers. You have to be careful, Kyle. If she is winning, she'll start cheating. Even though she is grown up on the outside, Mecca is still a child on the inside. When she was little, she loved to play, but the other children would not play with her. So, she uses the Magical Door to play with any child she wants. She knows that once they enter the Magical Door, they have no choice but to play with her. Bumblebyia used to be full of children, and it was such a happy place. Someone has to beat her and make Bumblebyia happy again."

Kyle heard a loud noise. He turned and saw the Mooky Booky tribe running toward them. "Thelma!" he yelled. "Which way is the Rainbow Castle?" "You'll have to go through the Crazy Cave," Thelma said and pointed to the Crazy Cave.

Kyle yelled, "Here comes the Mooky Booky tribe. We have to go." Kyle and his friends ran into the Crazy Cave where they saw eight different tunnels. Kyle said, "There are too many tunnels. We are going to have to split up." When they entered the Cave, they walked inside of a cave and heard loud laughing. They saw different colored crazy blinking lights. They each ran into a tunnel to separate. Kyle knew the Mooky Booky tribe was after the candy in his pocket. Kyle ducked into a zig-zag tunnel. He saw ladders leading up to other tunnels. Smelly was being chased by Mooky Booky tribe members, so he came out of one tunnel and went into another. Leapy ran through a tunnel with Beanie in his pouch. Doe Doe ran past them with two Mooky Booky tribe members chasing him. The blinking lights made it hard for him to see. Kyle ran out of one tunnel and saw another tunnel. Kyle went into the tunnel, but it was like a hillside. Kyle had to climb to get away from the Mooky Booky tribe. Smelly was running in another tunnel, and ran past Leapy with Beanie in his pouch. Doe Doe lost the Mooky Booky tribe members who were chasing him, and he was able to escape from the Crazy Cave. Leapy ran so fast he left the Mooky Booky tribe members in the dust. Leapy was lost at first but then he found his way out of the Crazy Cave.

Smelly ran back into a tunnel, and it took him all the way out of the Cave. Smelly, Leapy, Beanie, and Doe Doe were safe outside of the Crazy Cave. However, the Mooky Booky tribe kept chasing after Kyle. Kyle climbed higher and higher up the wall, but the Mooky Booky tribe members were right behind him. He saw something bright at the top of the wall. Kyle kept on climbing. He was very worried the Mooky Booky tribe members were going to catch up with him. When he reached the top of the wall, the Mooky Booky tribe members lost their grip and slipped and fell down the wall. Kyle climbed toward the light and out of the Crazy Cave. They had all made it out of the

Crazy Cave safely. Kyle looked ahead and saw a huge glass bridge that led to the Rainbow Castle.

Kyle grinned and said, "All we have to do is cross that bridge and we'll be at the beautiful Rainbow Castle."

When they began to walk across the bridge, Doe Doe looked down and became very scared. The Great Taffy River raged below them. "I can't go," he said. "I'm too scared. My feet won't move. Help me, I'm shaking like a leaf."

"Don't look down, Doe Doe," Smelly said.

"Are you afraid of heights?" Leapy asked.

"Yes, I am," Doe Doe said.

"Close your eyes and we'll hold your hands," Kyle said.

So Kyle and Smelly held Doe Doe's hands. Doe Doe couldn't see the raging Great Taffy River, but he could hear it. The River echoed loudly beneath them, which frightened him even more than seeing it. "I want my mommy," he said.

"Your mommy is far away," Leapy replied. "And she would just tell you to march up to your room if she knew where you were going."

Finally, the gang reached the end of the Glass Bridge and walked up to the Rainbow Castle door.

However, the Castle did not have a doorknob or a doorbell. "How are we supposed to get into the castle with no door knob?" Smelly asked. Kyle looked at the side of the door and saw a hammer next to a block with a weight with a bell above it. Kyle had seen games like this before, if you hit the block hard enough to send the weight up high enough to ring a bell, you won a prize.

He said, "I wonder if the doors will open if I hit the block with the hammer." He decided to take a chance and he picked up the hammer and hit the block hard. But the weight only went half way up and did not reach the bell. Kyle took the hammer and hit the block again. The weight went up even higher, but it still did not reach the bell.

"Hit it with all your might, Kyle," Smelly said.

Kyle took the hammer and lifted it high. He slammed the hammer down hard on the block. The weight flew up and rang the bell. The Rainbow Castle doors opened.

Nervously, Kyle and his friends entered the Castle. They walked down a large hallway. Kyle said, "I'm getting goose bumps, and I have butterflies in my stomach."

Doe Doe said, "I didn't know you like to eat butterflies!" They all laughed.

As they walked down the large hallway, they saw a roller coaster at the end of it. "Wow! A roller coaster!" Kyle said. "I've got to ride on it."

They all hopped into seats on the roller coaster. A lap bar secured them. The roller coaster started to move really fast. Kyle held onto the bar tightly as they went through a tunnel. Then the roller coaster went down a steep slope and into a double loop. Then it slowed down and came to a complete stop.

Kyle looked at his friends. "Now that was so much fun, I want to get back on for another ride. I love to ride roller coasters," he said.

Smelly frowned. "No, Kyle, we have to keep going. If you stop to play, Mecca will declare that you have forfeited the games. Then she will win." Kyle thought about what Smelly had said.

"Your right, Smelly," he said. "I've got some games to play."

They got off of the roller coaster and walked down another large hall.

"Look out!" Smelly yelled. They saw giant father shoes walking down the hall. The shoes almost stomped on Kyle and his friends. They waited for the perfect time to run. As soon as one of the shoes went up, they ran to a safe spot. However, the next father shoe was stomping too fast. Kyle had to time the shoe just right or they would be smashed underneath it. Kyle carefully watched the shoe. It went up and down three times. Once the father shoe went up for the fourth time, Kyle said, "Let's go, right now!" They all ran and dove away from the father shoes. When the shoes were gone, Kyle got up and said, "That was a close one."

They all walked to the end of the hall and turned the corner. They saw six colorful crayons moving up and down. "Oh, no," Kyle said. "Not again."

Kyle knew they had to be careful. Like the father shoes, The giant crayons were capable of smashing them. The first giant crayon came down. They quickly ran past it and it went back up. "I don't know if we're going to survive this one," Kyle said.

"Just tell us when to go, and we'll run," Leapy said.

Kyle was in front. He waited for the second giant crayon to go up. However, as soon as Kyle began to step forward, the giant crayon came down quickly. Kyle jumped back fast.

"What are we going to do?" asked Doe Doe.

"When the crayon hits the floor, we'll run," Kyle replied.

The giant crayon came down and Kyle yelled, "Make a run for it!" The giant crayon went up and they ran past it.

"What a plan!" Leapy said. "We made it!"

Getting past the next three giant crayons was easy, but the last giant crayon came down with a lot of force. They waited to see what would happen next.

Kyle let the last giant crayon go up and down three times. The fourth time the giant crayon went up, he yelled, "Let's go!" and they ran past it without even getting scratched.

Doe Doe sighed and said, "I'm glad that's over with."

"You said it!" Smelly said.

They began to walk down the hallway. The non-sculls were at the end, waiting for Kyle and his friends. Kyle said, "We'll have to run past them really fast so they don't catch us." They ran past the non-sculls, but the non-sculls began to chase them down the hallway.

Kyle said, "Smelly, hurry! Send out a stink bomb."

Smelly frowned, "I can't do it!"

"Yes, you can, Smelly. Try really hard," Kyle cheered.

Smelly turned around and saw the non-sculls coming toward them. He screamed and let out a stink bomb. The non-sculls stopped and fanned the air while holding their noses.

"Good job, Smelly! I knew you could do it," Kyle said.

Kyle and his friends continued to walk down the hallway. Kyle saw a big gift box on the floor. His eyes lit up. "That's the biggest gift I've ever seen," he said. I wonder what's in it. Maybe it's a robot or a truck."

Smelly spotted a cage above the big gift box. "No! Get away from there. It's a trap," he cried. Suddenly, the cage fell. Smelly pushed Kyle out of the way and Smelly got trapped inside of the cage. Leapy, Doe Doe, and Kyle all tried to lift the cage, but the cage was too heavy.

Leapy said, "Don't worry Smelly. We'll get you out of there."

Doe Doe shook his head, "I don't think so," he said.

Smelly started to panic. "Please do something. I can't stay in here."

The gang tried again to lift the cage and free their friend, but the cage was just too heavy.

"We have to get him out of there," Kyle said. "Smelly we're going to save you, just you wait and see."

Then, all of a sudden, Mecca's evil laugh filled the hallway. "That's Mecca," Leapy said and started to shake. "She must be close by."

"We're going to get it now," Beanie said. Just then, two big doors across from them opened up. Kyle and his friends could see a large game room inside of the doors.

"Are you going in there, Kyle?" Leapy said.

"That must be where Mecca wants me to go, but we can't leave Smelly out here alone."

"Kyle, don't worry about me, go ahead and beat the Evil Queen. I'll be all right," Smelly said. "Please, Kyle, you have to go."

So Kyle, Leapy, Doe Doe, and Beanie went into the big doors. Two of the Mooky

Booky tribe members closed the large doors behind them. Many Figets, Difaddos, and Masked People were there to watch the games. Beebee, the two-headed monster, greeted Kyle. "Hi, my name is Beebee. Be prepared to play the games that the Evil Queen Mecca has selected. Queen Mecca is the best in Bumblebyia, and she wishes to challenge you in her three favorite games. If you win the games, Queen Mecca will open the Magical Door and you may leave. If you don't win the games, you will be her prisoner forever and you can never leave. Are you ready?"

"I'm ready to give it my all," Kyle said.

Beebee turned to the crowd and announced: "We have a challenge, Queen Mecca and Kyle. They shall play three games. May the best one win. Let me proudly introduce to you the champion of all time, Queen of Bumblebyia, Mecca the Beautiful!"

Mecca appeared from behind the curtain. Everyone clapped as she entered the Royal Game Room.

Mecca walked up to Kyle and introduced herself. "I'm Mecca, Queen of Bumblebyia. And you must be the legend who will lose to me. I have never lost a challenge. You will soon be my prisoner. And, by the way, did you have a nice trip here?" Mecca threw her head back and laughed loudly.

"I'll just have to do my best," Kyle said, "because I refuse to stay here and be your prisoner."

Mecca raised her eyebrows, laughed, and said, "Get ready to lose, buddy."

Beebee shouted, "Let the games begin! The first game will be the water-gun race."

When Mecca started to walk toward the water-gun race, she tripped over a wire and stumbled.

Kyle laughed and said, "Did *you* have a nice trip?"

"Very funny," replied Mecca.

Kyle and Queen Mecca took their places. The clowns were set in place.

Beebee said, "Get ready, get set, go!"

Kyle and Mecca began to spray the targets to send their clowns toward the finish line. Mecca sprayed her target right in the middle, but Kyle kept missing his target. Mecca's clown got a head start because Kyle's clown kept stopping. Mecca's clown was half-way up when Kyle started to aim directly at his target. Kyle aimed perfectly and his clown shot up quickly, but Mecca's clown was already at the finish line.

Mecca jumped up and down and shouted, "Yes! I won! I won!" The crowd cheered for

Evil Queen Mecca. But Kyle refused to give up.

Mecca looked at Beebee and said, "This is going to be a piece of cake. Kyle doesn't have a chance."

Beebee turned to the crowd and said, "Next, they will play the ring-toss game. Whoever gets the most rings on the neck of the bottle wins. Each player will get six tries. Kyle, you'll go first."

Kyle stepped up to the line and took a deep breath. He was feeling nervous because he had already lost the first game. "This is a hard game to play," he said.

He looked at all the bottles lined up in rows and tossed his first ring. The ring hit one of the bottles, but bounced off of it.

Mecca said, "Ha ha, nice try. You're just a kid who is in way over his head."

Kyle ignored Mecca, and looked at the bottles carefully. He aimed and threw his second ring. The ring landed around the neck of the bottle.

He threw the third ring, and it popped off one bottle and landed on another. The crowd cheered.

Mecca said, "That was just luck."

Kyle tossed the fourth ring, he made it! He realized he only had two rings to go. He tossed the fifth ring and made it. Everyone in the royal game room was silent as Kyle picked up and tossed his last ring. The ring hit a bottle, and landed around the neck of another one.

Mecca said, "Five out of six, I can beat that." Beebee handed Mecca six rings. "Move back and give me some space," she sneered. Mecca tossed the first ring. It fell between the bottles. She frowned. She took the second ring and tossed it, this one went around the neck of a bottle. Her third ring also landed around the neck of a bottle, as did her fourth ring. "Yes!" she said, "I'm on a roll." She took the fifth ring and tossed it. It, too, went around the neck of a bottle.

Beebee said, "You haven't lost your touch, you are truly the best."

"Thank you Beebee."

Mecca smiled as she tossed the last ring. The ring hit three bottles and fell.

Beebee said, "Kyle wins the ring toss game by one ring."

Mecca yelled, "How can it be? I always win this game."

Beebee said, "The last game will be the basketball challenge. You both get five shots each. Each of you has a win. The one with the most shots will be the champ. Mecca, the Queen of Bumblebyia, will start the game."

"It'll be my pleasure to start," said Mecca. "This is history in the making."

Mecca took the first ball, and made a hook shot. Mecca shot her second ball, and smiled when she made the shot. "I am *so* good at this," she said.

Mecca shot her third ball, and the basketball went in. Her fourth ball hit the backboard and went into the hoop. She aimed her last ball, shot, but the ball bounced on the rim and fell away from the basket.

"No!" Mecca said. "I always make five in a row."

"Now it's Kyle's turn to shoot," Beebee said. Kyle walked up to the line.

Kyle took his first ball and shot it. The ball hit the backboard, then fell into the hoop. Kyle's second ball hit all net. The third did the same. Kyle had a good feeling about his next two shots. He made this fourth shot, and his fifth shot hit the backboard, went around the rim three times, and fell in.

The crowd cheered for Kyle.

Mecca said, "Since I'm the champ, I demand my bonus shot. Step to the side, you chump."

Kyle backed away and gave the ball to Mecca. "This is cheating," he said.

Mecca smiled and said, "This shot will put the game away."

Mecca shot the basketball and missed, but the ball hit the rim and made the court crooked. "*Oops,* look at what I did," she said. "What a pity! And I think it's still your turn."

"This is definitely cheating," Kyle asserted. Kyle took the last ball to throw in the basket, but the basketball court was still crooked. Still, Kyle tried to take aim at the court.

"I'll bet my powers that he won't make it," Mecca said.

Kyle thought about his own basketball court back home. It was also crooked. He shot the ball and the ball went in. Swoosh!

Mecca's face burned red. "No!" she shouted. Within seconds, her magic powers disappeared.

Leapy, Beanie, and Doe Doe cheered loudly because Kyle won the game. A big rainbow appeared across Bumblebyia. The Figets, Difaddos, and Masked People all cheered. They were all happy because Kyle won the games.

Mecca put her head in her hands and whined, "I don't believe he made that shot." Then the Rainbow Soldier's Statue came to life and the Rainbow Soldiers came to take Mecca and Beebee away.

The non-sculls and the Mooky Booky tribe were free from Mecca's evil spell. Everyone celebrated as balloons and confetti fell from the sky. Kyle and Doe Doe found the giant key and opened the prison door.

They set all the children Mecca had held captive free. The children were very happy to see Kyle and to be free.

Smelly ran into the Royal Game Room and said, "Congratulations Kyle. I knew you could do it."

Kyle looked surprised. He said, "Smelly, how did you get out?"

"The cage lifted off me as soon as Mecca lost her powers."

Cootie saw Kyle and asked, "How was your—"

"It was amazing!" Kyle blurted out before Cootie had a chance to finish.

Then Kyle said, "Cootie, you said the Rainbow Castle was only two blocks away."

Cootie just smiled.

Miss Tuweeni said, "Since you won the games, Kyle, you have activated the candy. Now you can give one piece to each child." Kyle passed out the candy. The children unwrapped the candy and ate it. Then, many Magical Doors appeared. All the children started to wave goodbye to everyone in the land of Bumblebyia as they walked through the doors.

Kyle looked at his friends sadly. "Before I wanted to leave," he said, "but now I don't want to go. I had so much fun, and I got a chance to make new friends. I don't think I should eat this piece of candy, but since I'm really hungry, I'll just put it in my mouth."

Cootie said, "Wait Kyle, here's a trophy for you. You are the new champion of Bumblebyia." The trophy had "Number One Champion, Kyle" written on it.

"Thank you for the trophy," Kyle said.

Kyle unwrapped the piece of candy, and put it in his mouth. Then his Magical Door appeared. Leapy, Beanie, Smelly, and Doe Doe cried as they said goodbye to Kyle. Kyle sadly waved goodbye to his special friends. Then Kyle went through the door.

Two months later:

Kyle sat in his new classroom on the first day of school. His teacher greeted the class. "Hi!" she said. "I'm Ms. Jones. Since it's the first day of school, let's talk about the summer. Tell me what you did that was exciting this summer."

Kyle's classmate Tammy raised her hand and Ms. Jones told her to come to the front of the room. "My name is Tammy Bigler and for my summer vacation I went to Buddy World Amusement Park," Tammy said and smiled. "I got on all of the rides. My friends and I played games and won prizes. I had a lot of fun this summer." Tammy sat down.

Ms. Jones called another student to the front of the room. "Hi," the boy said. "My name is Robert Mills. I went to summer camp this summer. We went hiking, fishing, and horseback riding. I came in second place in a pie-eating contest. After summer camp I went on a trip to Buddy World Amusement Park." Robert took his seat.

Next Ms. Jones called Kyle to the front of the room. Kyle smiled and introduced himself to Ms. Jones. "I was in my room this summer when suddenly a large door appeared. There was a neon sign over the top of the door that read, "A Great Vacation Spot." I didn't have any place to go for the summer, so I walked through the door. There was a whole different world on the other side called Bumblebyia where all the children can play. I made some very special friends there—Leapy the kangaroo, Smelly the skunk, Beanie the koala bear, and Doe Doe the clown. I also made other friends who were called Figets and Difaddos. They baked a giant cake for me and it wasn't even really my birthday. We played games and had lots of fun. Then the Evil Queen Mecca closed the Magical Door. My friends and I had to go to the Rainbow Castle where I challenged the Evil Queen Mecca in three games. I had to collect candy on my way to the Rainbow Castle. A giant crab and three mean ducks chased us. I also met a big peacock named Thelma. My friends and I crossed a glass bridge, and entered the Rainbow Castle. I defeated the Evil Queen Mecca and she lost her powers.

Then the statues of the Rainbow Soldiers came to life. They took the Evil Queen Mecca away, and I rescued all the kids, who lost against Mecca and were kept prisoners. I gave them all a piece of candy to eat. Once they ate the candy, their own Magical Doors appeared, and the kids went home. I didn't want to go back home, but I did miss my family and my friends. So I ate a piece of the candy and went through the Magical Door. A tear dropped from Kyle's eyes.

A little girl in the front row said, "You're a hero, Kyle." The rest of the class chanted, "He-ro, he-ro."

Ms. Jones said, "Enough class, calm down. We know Kyle is a hero, but Kyle, weren't the kids you saved on their *vacation*?"

Kyle grinned and said, "Yes, but some vacations are longer than others." Then the whole class laughed.

The End

Bumblebyia Theme Song

by Miliki Fisher

The Magical Door

In the land where friends

are many

And adventure is fun

and plenty

In my dreams I go to places

where there are smiles on

lots of faces

As I close my eyes and

make wishes

I see water clouds and

pretty fishes

M. Y. Fisher

In the village we're all buddies

We like candy and silly putty

There is yellow skies and trees that are blue

Happy Figets and Difaddos

It's a special place all kids desire

And the name is Bumblebyia

Bumblebyia (chorus)

Apple pie-a

Jumble lyia

Bumblebyia

Bumblebyia (chorus)

Pacifier

Apple pie-a

Bumblebyia

Bumblebyia (chorus)

Scooba diva

Don't ask why-a

Bumblebyia

Bumblebyia (chorus)

Pumkin pie-a

Candy buy-a's

Bumblebyia

By Miliki Fisher

About the Author

Miliki Fisher was born in Philadelphia, Pennsylvania. He grew up in the Passyunk homes. He went to the schools in South Philadelphia. He has a wife of eleven years and four children. Miliki Fisher loved to draw cartoon characters. He began to draw at the age of five. In school Miliki made posters and book report covers for his fellow classmates. At lunchtime the kids used to sit around and watch him draw. He also entered into drawing contests. Certificates and Awards were given to him for his artwork. Miliki would draw cartoons for hours at home. But, he wanted to make the cartoons talk. Just like the cartoons on TV, so he began to make illustrations. He would draw balloons and write words in them. He would have the cartoons talk to one another. Miliki started to create his own cartoons. He was making his own comic books. In the sixth grade he ran for class president. He drew up all the posters to help him win. At the age of twelve years old he joined a DJ Group.   He did block parties, Birthday parties, and Weddings in his neighborhood. At that time music was a big part of his life. But, drawing was more important. He saw a group of people painting walls. They were cleaning up graffiti in the city. The city was hiring kids for the summer. So he signed up for the Anti-Graffiti Program.   He worked with Anti-Graffiti painting walls. Then he began to paint murals. He was in the Program for four years. Miliki took interest in his writings and he began to do more writing and less drawing. Miliki has been writing short stories and Novels for fifteen years.